PÈLÚMI

LOVE LETTERS & HEART RAMBLINGS

LOVE LETTERS & HEART RAMBLINGS

Love LETTERS & HEART Ramblings
Pèlúmi Obasaju

ISBN: 9781919608501
eISBN: 9781919608518

Cover Design: Michaella Saineti
Illustrator: Destiny Sanyaolu
Videographer: Crystal Carless & Joakin Okeke

First Printing, 2021

CONTENTS

CONTENTS

To Love In All Its Forms
To The One Who Is Love

WRENCHES & WINDOWS

I'm learning to be more open
Constructing wrenches rather than walls
Embracing the fear and discomfort
That comes with entrusting grenades and bullets
To those I allow a glimpse into my soul
I grab their hands
Willing them not to let go
As I be summer tour guide
Plastered smile
Steps centred on their experience
They run through my mind
Skipping over each gyrus and fold
Over perfectly placed triumphs
Dusting past the mementos and victory plaques
To the backdrops
The clutter that props it all up
Taking hold
That they may bear witness to my inner depths

SCAN ME | password:
windows

L

Have you ever seen the letter of love?
Marvelled at its freedom
Its zealous audacity
Its childlike glee
The smile it easily evokes as it is just
As it just
IS
Just
IS
Purposefully at ease

A THUGS LOVE POEM

Here's my attempt at a love poem
I'm just going to start off the blocks with: your heart is deep
I think they lied in geography class when they said that
the oceans were the deepest areas on earth
They should have added the caveat on your heart
It's Challenger Deep
Requiring Holy Spirit guidance
to explore and steward the light and shade
To not oversimplify your emotions and render you 2D
Every dimension deserves thought and care
So, yeah
Your heart is deep
I'll leave it there
From an undercover romantic in a thug exterior

SCAN ME | password:
thug

ON TRUE INTIMACY

I'm committed to learn you
And you desire to learn me
Today's my last day of freedom
I'm glad I spent it with you

You are worth learning
We take our time
Exploring each other

Prodding and poking tentatively
Seeing how much
How far we'd let the other in
Intimacy is unveiling my soul to you
Being comfortable enough to let you love me in my weakness
Sharing with you parts of me no one else has ever seen
Trust is at the heart of intimacy

Do I trust you?
Do you trust me?
You seemed unafraid of the unknown
But I guess the brave feel fear too

O

To love is a choice
With feelings attached, To love
Is everything for
God is everything
And God is love

RANDOM THOUGHTS AT 00:00

I like to tell myself stories
Make believe myself into the truth that love will fall into me
again
My fairy tale is on self-discovery
On knowing my worth
On knowing my worth to be loved
On enjoying the folds of my mind
On process and possibilities
Embracing and enjoying the endless potential for
joy and passion
This bedtime story is on me falling in love with
me
Taking a leap in this world full of beauty
Believing I am one of the beautiful things filling
this world

00:07

Is part of enjoying the folds of my mind pacing
these cobbled paths?
Winding through the wastelands of broken
dreams?

What was
What could have been
Weeping at what is

We're all foreigners in this forbidden land

Strangers
Trying to make our mark
Trying to stake our claim in the annuals of time
Darting full force
Trying to find our meaning

We pray for this forbidden land to find its meaning

TODAY

_____

Today I tried to write about happiness
Tried to exorcise the cloud of gloom inked into
my soul
Tried to reconstruct that carefree feeling of my
youth

You know the one

Little you running through a playground
Or a field of daffodils
Or maybe daisies
The scene a sienna hue
Or a jasper filter

Did I mention that the running is probably in
slo-mo
With your smile as wide as [insert cliché here]

I tried to write about that feeling of joy
That contentment felt in moments of bliss
Tried to distract myself from the cold current of
my predicament
Tried to exercise my fingers to play a tune less
melancholic

Today I tried to write about happiness

But I stopped

Realising that my moments of joy were ever
more joyful because I had experienced the tears
of heartbreak

That the moments I had been grateful
Full of contentment
And heartfelt thanks
Were due to my experiencing the complete
opposite

I stopped
And embraced this bittersweet epiphany
For all it was worth
Let it reconstruct the lens in which I viewed my
sadness

Laughed as I uttered
"Better days are coming"
The tears may last for this moment but joy will
surely come
Surely my joy will come

AN ATTEMPT AT PRAYER

_____

They say You are the mender of broken hearts
Forgive me for the hearts I've broken as You
unbreak mine
You lead me beside still waters
But these rivers don't stop
These salt laced missives speak of what my lips
can't utter
Do Your paths of righteousness extend to my
calcified heart?
As I fluctuate from praise to anger
Hand stitched questions with a happiness core
My cup overflowing uncontrollably
In the presence of my enemies
As oil, snot and tears marry
Forgive me for the hearts I've broken as You
unbreak mine

SWEET

We embraced under the bubble-gum refrain
Lost in our delusions that this moment won't
melt away
We shared random thoughts
Clouded in a sugar rush of trust
Marvelling at the canvas that tented us
That backdropped and framed our reality

UNDER THE ORANGE TREE

Our mouths are sweet
Our bodies are well
We double-dutch through each ray
Expertly contorting our bodies
To the opening of warmth
Careful not to get burnt

Under the orange tree
Is where we play our games
Singing rhymes our mothers passed down
on
cushioned knees

SCAN ME | password:
orange

Our mouths are sweet
Our bodies are well
As we savour each misplaced word
Lábẹ́ igi òròṁbó

THE PICTURE

My cheeks were freshly fried puff puffs
Glowing orbs of playground mischief and
lunchtimes of hopscotch and handclap games
Of Mary Mack and Tic Tac Toe

High

                                  Low
       Chicka Low

Was how each strand danced out of the barrettes
    Mama had carefully placed that morning

Her eyes stare back at me

Little me

So unconcerned

       Exploring

           Engrossed

In every inch of whatever life presented

Her eyes stare back at me
Little me
So unconcerned
Exploring
Engrossed

        Mind the gap between my simple
        freedom and my dawn of hyper
           awareness

7 OR 8

---

7 or 8 was when it began
No tears were shed
It's funny how that's my earliest memory now
Delay tactics disguised as bedtime snack requests
Anything for that extra time
Anything for those moments of cut crusts and
planted kisses
It's funny the details my mind zooms in on
The contents of that Pandora's envelope
No fight
Just flight
Frozen
Numb to the initial wound
As the emotional keloid formed a foundation to
my tolerance of abandonment
No tears were shed
When Daddy left
Overcompensation rooted in pain
Refusing to be another story of lament
Added to the anthology of daddy's girls with
Daddy's issues

FOR YOUR SMILE

How I wished it was preserved
Protected and wrapped in cotton
Wooled from a world that prejudged
before truly getting to know you

We faced it as soon as we entered the system
How they treated you compared to me
How they mistakened your black boy joy for restlessness
Your curiosity for trouble
They dubbed you trouble before you spoke a word

I remember how a white "friend" in primary
tried to get on to you
The lion in me came out
That was before your growth spurt
Before you towered over me
Before the world viewed you as fetish or threat

It's hard letting go
Hard knowing I can't protect you as I want to
Hard seeing your smile disappear
As the hard knocks of life
don't take the time to know your genius

You'll always be my little brother
No matter how small my frame is to your teddy bear stance
My fierceness is enough for the both of us
I miss the days they used to mistaken us as twins
Miss the closeness

I can't miss this moment
Any moment
To say
"I love you"

I want my " I love you" to be your cotton wool
To illicit that deep smile that lights up your whole being
Let my "I love you" resonate and remind you of you
Not who "they" dub you to be

It's hard accepting my "I love you" may not be enough
But
I'll forever try

IN MEMORIAM

To the ghost of what could have been
The vapours were oh so sweet
I selah'd in the perfect imaginings
Dancing to the key of life untainted

To the doors that should have remained
unopened
But intrigue got us unlatching unhealed wounds
Widening each bruise and welding them in well
wishes and platitudes

I'll address this one to the insecurities
The ones you dug up rather messily
The skeletons you shook
The capsule of commitment
That was a forget-me-not to my future self

To the potential that was thriving in toxicity
Rooted in unanswered questions
All-consuming in all the wrong ways
&&
You probably don't care

BLEEDING OUT

I will no longer bleed out for you
No longer lay my wounds on the stage of your
amusement
Dispensing my soul for your entertainment
Hoping you feel
Something
Hoping that empathy is birthed
And compassion be the fruit
Of a heart steeped revelation of true love
Not that parasitic love the movies spin
But let ours be a symbiosis
A union of mutuals
Striding to eternity
Let this dream crown
Let me take my stand
Love me enough to tend to these open wounds
Respect me enough to heal in the secret place
Allow these antiseptic tears cleanse the debris
As I lay me before the throne room of grace
This saving grace teaching me to feel healthily again

00:08

We pace these cobbled paths

Winding through the wastelands of our broken dreams

What was

What could have been

What is

This forbidden land
This new beginning
Now queries *us*
Us wanderers
Us dreamers
Us pilgrims alike

What do **you** represent?

FIRST STEPS

I feel it creeping in
Silently encroaching the space formerly occupied
by me

Well the old me
Not this shell you now see
Devoid of emotions
Desperately trying to salvage
And cling to what once was

Putting on the face of
"I'm good, how about you"
Even dishing out advice and comforting others

The life of the crowd
Cracking people up as I walk the room
Work the room
A caricature of who I once was

Desperately picking up the pieces of the
damaged mask

Forcing them to fit together with my special brand of
superglue called smile

Cause a smile fixes everything right?

"You can let us in you know"
But do they really want to know?
The suffocating episodes on repeat
"We're here for you, you know"
Will you stay put?
"You don't have to talk,
just know I'm here to listen when you're ready"
"Just know I'm here when you are ready"

Their annoyingly persistent love
Brushes and blows away my glittered vagueness
Floodlighting my hope and future
Guiding me to face the root
To see the beauty in the collage of me

An Accepting
An utterance whispered to God and community
A realising that I held the keys to my release

It was taking the first steps that were the hardest
"I need help"

SOME REASONS

After 'Mountain Dew Commercial Disguised as a Love Poem'
by Matthew Olzmann

Because of British summers spent camping in the
rain in sliding tents
Laughing hysterically at Pepe and other things
not funny without context
Because you wear truth on a chain of love but
cuss me out as quickly for my overthinking
Because we can cry, be frustrated and bare our
hearts about things during our catch ups
To be very honest, we can't always fully articulate
ourselves
Yet we still understand without all the words
being packaged right
You listen
And as you say a good listener is a golden friend

Because you love food and love your friends
So depending on the season we could be dubbed
anything from angel cake to chicken

You came to see me the night before I left
You came to see me when I was in a weird
headspace
Because you've stuck around when my walls
were up and I go into defence mode

SCAN ME | password:
reasons

You are persistent

We challenge each other in faith and life
Even though we've had bumps along the way
We can press play and there is no awkwardness

Because this is a friendship open to footnotes
and reviews and we can speak our minds freely
We're still figuring things out and
accommodating to the fact we are growing and
evolving and at times not sure where this is going
Because we've survived the growing pains of
different stages
From preteen crushes to whatever season this is

Because we can argue and debate and agree to disagree
Because you don't take life too seriously
And we can laugh hysterically at songs like
Baby Got Back on streets like Butt Close Lane
Because this hasn't been 11 or 12 or 13 years of
friendship for no reason
So you're not getting rid of me
That's what I've got, why this might just work

TO DO #1

What do you do when you're in a season of pain?

When you're prone to slipping into a dark space

But believe in a God who does the impossible

What do you do when you're rooted in faith

But you're dealt with sucker punch after sucker
punch in a short space of time
What do you do?

V

Today I asked God a question drenched in
self-pity and rooted in doubt
He responded so softly through pockets of
wisdom stitched into moments, conversations
and encounters
That the grace to breathe in the air of a
brand-new day
To feel the warmth of the sun against this vessel
of clay
That my lungs ability to beat in sync with my
intercostal muscles
Dancing with my diaphragm to oxygenate my
blood
Which traverses intricately to sustain this hunk of
neural matter
Triggering the synaptic response
To formulate and utter
The question
Was evidence of His favour
Of His Grace
Of Him gifting me with life
And now the choice lay with me

TO DO #2

To walk in obedience

To tune into the frequency of His heart

Speak of God boldly

Pray and declare your love for Him

Admitting that things aren't alright won't
discourage others

Realise that God can use these broken pieces to
display even more of Him

Open up to God
Let Him in on ALL of it
He can handle it
Deep it and see His hand upon it all
See His fingerprint and signature of love all over it

E

To finding my voice again
Sitting in this bespoke void
Balancing the silence with each breath

Getting my fill of daily bread
I weigh in
Allow the Master Tailor to have free reign

A cut here
A seam there
Darts and pleats that most won't see

He whispers the fabric unto the skin of my heart

Lightly bastes in the laughter of loved ones
Each moment
Ornately fashioned
Delicately powerful
Giving me the language to go on

WILL YOU ANSWER THE CALL TO LOVE?

Even in the midst of heartbreak
Will you answer the call to love?

As you wade through the shattered pieces of
your tear stained memories

Will you answer the call to love?

Not the auditory candy floss of their sweet
nothings

Whispered in the dead of night

Dissipating in the light of day

Each sand of time echoing the ever-growing
distance

Between them

and the truth of what love is

Will you answer the call to Love?

Will you respond?

Utter your response
With sincerity of breath
A heartfelt cry to replace your flawed version of love
With His

Will you answer the call to Love?

Will you answer the call of Love?

That existed before time was
That loved you at your worst
That Love

SCAN ME

Better than a fairy tale
That Love
That eternal truth
God's love

NOTES

1. *Gyrus* from **'Wrenches & Windows'** is a neuroscience term referring to the ridges between the anatomical grooves of the brain.
2. *Challenger Deep* from **'A thugs love poem'** is the deepest known point in the Earth's seabed hydrosphere.
3. *Lábẹ́ igi òròmbó* from **'Under the orange tree'** is a Yorùbá song and phrase meaning 'under the orange tree'.
4. *Puff puff* from **'The Picture'** is a traditional African snack made of fried dough. *Mary Mack, Tic Tac Toe,* and *High Low Chicka Low* all refer to playground clapping games.
5. The commonly misused word *mistakened* in **'For Your Smile'** has been purposely used, as the urban dictionary puts it "You're not a word, but you've fooled a lot of people into thinking you are!". Take from this what you will.
6. *Selah'd* from **'In Memoriam'** refers to the Biblical exclamation occurring in the Psalms and the Book of Habakkuk. It means "pause and reflect upon ".
7. *Cuss* from **'Some Reasons'** refers to the slang word for insulting someone.

ACKNOWLEDGMENTS

First and foremost **Soli Deo Gloria.**

Many thanks to Mama, Tami, my family, friends and community.

Those who took time to advise, tell the truth and honestly steer me because they recognised something I did not.

Special shout out (in no particular order) to Ayin Abegunde, Tolu Agbelusi, Delasi Adorkorbidji, Crystal Carless, Arianne Carless-Lock, Sholape Jegede, Joakin Okeke, Chantelle Phinda, Michaella Saineti, Destiny Sanyaolu, and Tisha Talabi.

This is a leap of faith, a why not.

An ode to the random thoughts that are gems and contributors to the process of being.

ABOUT THE AUTHOR

Pèlúmi is passionate about God, emotional and relational intelligence, and art in all its expressions. Her writing gives the **mess of life a poetic voice** whilst reflecting the heart of God with full authenticity. She is a poet, storyteller and PhD candidate in Neuroscience who does not like to be boxed in. An **Academic Aesthete** who has a love for both the arts and sciences, believing they shouldn't be separated but should inform each other.

Pèlúmi believes in seeing **beauty** in the **process** of **life**, as she feels the mess of the process is often underappreciated in our generation. Seeing beauty in the process means **growing** through it rather than going through it.

Twitter & Instagram: @pelums_o
Email: beautyandprocess@gmail.com